Marielle in Paris

Written by **Maxine Rose Schur**

Illustrated by **Jeanne B. de Sainte Marie**

Pomegranate **kids**
AGES 3 to 103!

Published by PomegranateKids®, an imprint of
Pomegranate Communications, Inc.
19018 NE Portal Way, Portland OR 97230
800 227 1428 · www.pomegranate.com

Pomegranate Europe Ltd.
'number three', Siskin Drive
Middlemarch Business Park
Coventry CV3 4FJ, UK
+44 (0)24 7621 4461 · sales@pomegranate.com

Pomegranate's mission is to invigorate, illuminate, and inspire through art.

To learn about new releases and special offers from Pomegranate, please visit
www.pomegranate.com and sign up for our e-mail newsletter. For all other queries,
see "Contact Us" on our home page.

This product is in compliance with the Consumer Product Safety Improvement Act
of 2008 (CPSIA) and any subsequent amendments thereto. A General Conformity
Certificate concerning Pomegranate's compliance with the CPSIA is available on our
website at www.pomegranate.com, or by request at 800 227 1428. For additional
CPSIA-required tracking details, contact Pomegranate at 800 227 1428.

Library of Congress Control Number: 2016961830

ISBN 978-0-7649-7935-4

Pomegranate Item No. A268

Designed by Carey Hall

Printed in China

26 25 24 23 22 21 20 19 18 17   10 9 8 7 6 5 4 3 2 1

In the heart of Paris lives a mouse named Marielle. Although she is smaller than a baby's fist, her ideas are big. Marielle is a dressmaker. She spends her days imagining fantastic clothes: a sweater with wings, a waterfall dress, a computer-screen coat.

At night, in her flowerpot home, she takes up needle and thread to make all that she has imagined.

One morning, Marielle heard a *tap-tap-tappety* at her door.

It was Madame de Sooree and her nine daughters, Berenice, Babette, Belle, Bernadette, Blanche, Blondelle, Brie, Brigitte, and Beatrice.

"Madame de Sooree!" exclaimed Marielle, "I am honored."

"Of course you are," replied Madame.

She and her nine daughters swept inside with their noses held high.

"In ten days, I am giving a very fancy party for my daughters' birthday," announced Madame de Sooree. "Marielle, I want you to create a new dress for each of my darlings."

"Ooh!" Marielle squeaked, "I will create the most beautiful dresses!"

"Of course you will," sniffed Madame.

"Come along, darlings."

Madame de Sooree turned and marched out the door with Berenice, Babette, Belle, Bernadette, Blanche, Blondelle, Brie, Brigitte, and Beatrice.

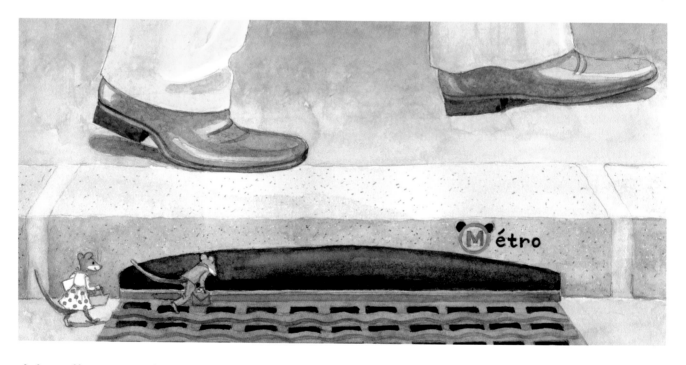

Marielle wasted no time. "For nine new dresses, I need nine new ideas!" In a wink she was out the door.

Marielle did not travel as many mice do, running along rooftops. Marielle feared high places so she stayed close to the ground. She scampered into the city where the sights would inspire her.

She looked at food in the market.

She laughed at a puppet show.

She sketched by the river.

She cooled off at a fountain.

She gazed at paintings.

She took tea with macarons.

She sailed on a boat.

She tickled a baby.

That evening, when the lights of the city glowed gold, Marielle hurried home, her mind bursting with ideas!

She worked far into the night. For nine days and nine nights she sketched, measured, pinned, cut, and stitched. At last, on the night before the party, she finished the dresses.

Satisfied with her work, she opened the window to let in the summer breeze. Then, tired but happy, she went to bed.

While she slept, the breeze turned into a wind. The dresses flapped and fluttered. The wind grew stronger. The dresses lifted into the air and flew around the room like colorful birds. *Whoosh!* They sailed out the window and vanished into the night.

The next morning, Marielle saw that all her dresses were gone.

She ran to her neighbor, Pierre.

"Pierre! The dresses I made for Madame de Sooree's daughters have vanished! I need to find them *tout de suite*! Can you help me?"

"*Oh là là!*" cooed Pierre. "Do not upset yourself. Crying makes your eyes too terribly tiny! Sit on my back, *ma petite*. We will fly above the city and find them."

"No, Pierre. I can't do that. I'm afraid of heights!"

"You must," he said. "We have so little time. It is the only way."

Marielle nodded. Taking a deep breath, she held tight to his silky feathers.

They zoomed into the wide, open sky.

Trembling with fear, Marielle dared to look down. Everything looked mouse-sized! They circled around the great cathedral of Notre-Dame.

"I see one!" cried Marielle.

Pierre swooped toward it. With one paw Marielle gripped Pierre's feathers, and with the other, she reached out and plucked the dress.

"Bravo!" said Pierre.

They found the second and third dresses close by.

They saw the fourth one twisting
in a tree.

They spotted the fifth one
just in time!

Pierre and Marielle glided above the Champs-Élysées. "Over there!"
She held on tight, took a deep breath and despite her fear, snatched the
sixth dress. Startled tourists dropped their ice creams.

"Humans!" said Pierre in disgust. "They are so messy!"

Marielle spied the seventh dress up high. Her heart pitter-pattered with fright, yet she mustered all the courage of a mouse and took it.

The eighth dress was right out in the open.

But where was the ninth dress?

They looked everywhere. Pierre and Marielle could not find it!

"Look!" Marielle squeaked. There, waving as proudly as the French flag, was the ninth dress.

"*Attention!*" called Pierre, racing toward it. Higher and higher and higher he flew. Marielle shut her eyes.

"Grab it!" Pierre cried.

"I can't, Pierre. I'm too scared!"

"Take it, Marielle. It is yours!"

Marielle shivered in terror. She was so awfully high—way up in the sky!
"It is mine," she told herself. "So I must take it!" She opened her eyes,
leaned forward, stretched out her tiny paw and . . .

. . . caught the ninth dress.

"I DID IT!" she shouted.

"*Magnifique!*" said Pierre.

But when she arrived home, Marielle's joy turned to panic. The ninth dress had snagged on the Eiffel Tower. It had a huge hole in it! Smack in the middle!

She had to deliver the dresses within minutes. There was no time to make another.

"Oh, I'm in trouble!" she cried. "Madame de Sooree will not be pleased!"

Marielle collapsed in tears. She cried her heart out.

Then a brilliant idea popped into her head.

Working quickly, she sewed big petals all around the hole. Voila! She had covered the ugly hole with a gorgeous flower!

When she delivered the dresses, Madame de Sooree was thrilled.

"These are the loveliest dresses in all Paris!" she pronounced, adding, "Marielle, your work shows the true refinement of the rodent."

Marielle blushed with pride.

"Come to the party tonight," Madame de Sooree said. "I want to show you off."

Bold with her new courage, Marielle asked, "May I bring my friend Pierre? He's very dear."

"You may," Madame replied. "I have seen your feathered friend in the garden—a gray, groomed individual—so distinguished."

It was a very fancy party!

Marielle and Pierre were greeted like honored guests.

In their colorful new dresses, Berenice, Babette, Belle, Bernadette, Blanche, Blondelle, Brie, Brigitte, and Beatrice twirled like tops around the dance floor.

And that night, in the heart of Paris, Marielle felt her own small heart burst with joy and pride.

Marielle's ideas for the nine party dresses and for her own party dress came from what she saw in Paris. Can you tell what inspired each dress? Look at the pictures again. They will tell you.

Then turn the page to check your answers.

PAGE 9

PAGE 9

PAGE 7

PAGE 8

PAGES 12–13

PAGE 7

PAGE 11

PAGE 7

PAGE 8

PAGE 10

Paris places and monuments shown in
Marielle in Paris

Note: On page 9, Marielle takes tea on a box of macarons from the historic Ladurée pastry shop.

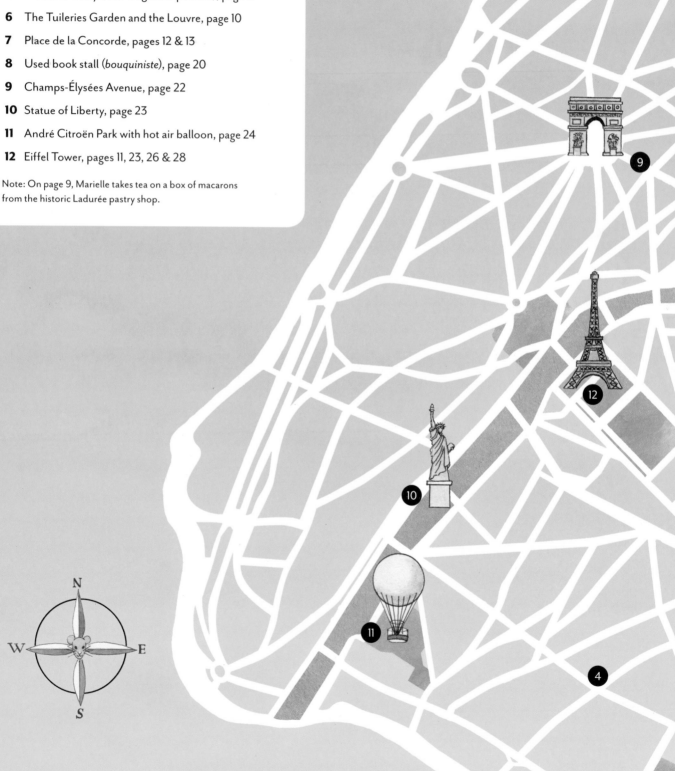